In memory of my beautiful friend and soul mom, Jeanne Fingerhut.
If I could, I would give you nine more lives, at very least.

With special thanks to Zara.

Art direction by Kristen Nobles.
Design by Mary Beth Fiorentino.
Typeset in Della Robbia.
The illustrations in this book were rendered in Holbein Acryla Gouache,
on Arches 140lb Hot Press watercolor paper.
Manufactured in Hong Kong.

Library of Congress Cataloging-in-Publication Data
Laden, Nina.
Romeow & Drooliet / Nina Laden.
p. cm.
Summary: A story of love between Romeow the cat and Drooliet the dog,
inspired by Shakespeare's tale of Romeo and Juliet, but with a happier ending.
ISBN 0-8118-3973-7
[1. Cats–Fiction. 2. Dogs–Fiction.] I. Title: Romeow and Drooliet .II. Title.
PZ7.L13735Rr 2004
[E]–dc22
2003017415

Distributed in Canada by Raincoast Books
9050 Shaughnessy Street, Vancouver, British Columbia V6P 6E5

10 9 8 7 6 5 4 3 2 1

Chronicle Books LLC
85 Second Street, San Francisco, California 94105

www.chroniclekids.com

Romeow & Drooliet

By Nina Laden

With a wag of the tale to William Shakespeare

chronicle books·san francisco

The Characters

The Felinis................A cat-loving family

The Barkers................A family of dog lovers

Romeow................The Felinis' favorite cat

Drooliet................The Barkers' cuddly canine

Benny................A Felini cat, brother and friend of Romeow

Marky................A Felini cat, brother and friend of Romeow

Turbo................The Barkers' guard dog

Mousignor................A church mouse

Officer Prince................Animal control warden

Other people, cats and dogs

Narrator................The one telling the story

BENNY

MARKY

Drooliet

Romeow

In the fair and sometimes not fair city,
There lived two nearby feuding families.
The Felinis were cat people, it's true.
They could not stand dogs or what those dogs do.
The dog-loving Barkers hated all cats.
Normally we would just leave it at that.
But we have a tale to tell of their pets.
A story of love. A tale of regret.
A story that has not quite started yet.
Now here is "Romeow and Drooliet."

Benny, Marky and Romeow were brothers, and the best of friends. One fine morning, they were taking a break from their naps.

"I'm bored," said Benny with a yawn.

"Let's go to the park," said Marky.

"What for?" asked Benny.

"To look for trouble," replied Marky.

"No," said Romeow, dreamily, "to look for love."

"Yuck," said Benny and Marky, "go back to sleep."

But Romeow was already on his way out the door with his tail held high.

The park was a great place for adventure. There were trees to climb, birds to chase and dogs to watch.

"Let's head to the off-leash area," Marky suggested.

"Can't catch me," he caterwauled to a large husky trapped behind the fence. "What do you think," he asked Romeow, "should we play Dodge Dog?"

Just as Romeow was about to reply, a carnivorous canine charged the cats. The hotheaded dog barked, snapped and nearly jumped the fence.

"Here, Turbo," someone called. "Come on, boy."

Turbo reluctantly left, and the cats decided that they should, too.

That was a close one," said Benny.

"Marky, one of these days you're going to get us into trouble," Romeow said, scowling.

"Come on, guys!" Marky replied. "There's a costume party in the neighborhood tonight. I hear they are having barbecued salmon and grilled shrimp. Shall we groom ourselves? What do you say?"

"I say we go home and get ready," Benny cheered.

"Okay, Marky, but no tricks," Romeow warned.

Come One
Come All
To Our
Costume Ball!
The Barkers
112 Bowser Avenue

Back at the Felini house, the cats dug through bags and drawers. When they were done, the room was as messy as a litter box. Dressed in their flashy finery, they streaked out the door like lightning and bolted into the night.

It was easy to find the party. Throngs of revelers, sounds of laughter and music and delicious smells spilled into the street.

"But that's the house of the cat-hating Barkers," Romeow protested.

"The sign says All Welcome," said Marky. "Besides, we're disguised."

"And I smell fish," Benny purred.

"I smell trouble," Romeow mumbled, looking at Marky.

But the Felini felines followed their noses. At least Benny and Marky did. Romeow followed his eyes. Gazing across the room, he thought he saw an angel. As he got closer, he felt warm all over. She was the most beautiful sight he had ever seen.

"May I have this dance?" Romeow nervously asked. He was delighted when she gave him her paw.

Door is Open.
All
Welcome!

As they danced, Romeow smiled. She smiled back. They twirled and dipped. The room spun. Romeow had never felt so happy. He looked at her collar.

"Drooliet, now there's a name that I'd drool over anytime," he said.

"And what shall I call you?" Drooliet panted.

But before Romeow could answer, Turbo, the terror from the park, growled from out of nowhere, "You can call him a freeloading Felini cat! Now scram before this party turns into a kitty catastrophe."

"My name is Romeow," Romeow called as he escaped. "We shall meet again, dear Drooliet."

"Not if I can help it," Turbo barked.

"Good boy," said the Barkers.

Romeow drifted through the Barkers' yard in a dreamy fog.
He couldn't get Drooliet out of his mind. Then suddenly,
he heard her voice coming from a balcony above.

"Oh, Romeow, where is that fur-faced Romeow?
I do not care that you are a cat or a Felini.
If you were a creature of any other name,
It would still make my tail wag."

With a running start, Romeow jumped onto the balcony
and landed next to Drooliet.

"Call me any name you want," Romeow purred,
    "just call me yours."

That moonlit night, cat and dog fell in love.

They had no cares, just the stars up above.

Romeow licked Drooliet on her face.

His whiskers tickled but she smiled with grace.

"We shall be married," said young Romeow.

"I'll be with you forever, starting now.

Meet me at the church. Sneak out of your house.

There we will be wed by Mousignor Mouse."

But will the world accept what happened next

To our dear Romeow and Drooliet?

They met the next day in front of the church. Romeow took Drooliet to a small chamber in the back. Mousignor Mouse entered, his robes flowing, his tail trailing.

"Are you ready to be joined together as husband and wife?" he squeaked.

"I will love you and fetch you anything you desire," Drooliet promised Romeow.

"I will love you and groom you even if I get hairballs," Romeow promised Drooliet.

"You may lick the bride," pronounced Mousignor Mouse.

All Beings Are Equal

Happily married, Romeow and Drooliet went for a walk in the park. The sky seemed bluer, the sun seemed brighter. Suddenly a large dark shadow ran towards them. It was Turbo!

"Drooliet, we've been looking for you. What are you doing with that cat?" he howled. "And you, Felini cat, will soon be puppy chow."

"Let's not fight," Romeow pleaded with Turbo, "we are family."

"No cat is kin to me," Turbo bellowed.

A crowd started to form. The Barkers arrived out of breath. Benny and Marky ran to Romeow's side.

"This is foolish," Benny told Romeow, "she's a dog. She's not worth it."

Marky hissed at Turbo, "Roll over and play dead, fleabag."

Turbo exploded and attacked Marky.

"Stop," cried Romeow, "it's me that you want."

Romeow drew his claws as Marky crawled away to lick his wounds. With all his might, Romeow swiped at Turbo's snarling, snapping, massive muzzle. In seconds, Turbo sank to the ground with barely a whimper.

"Cat got your tongue?" Benny taunted.

Romeow wanted to run to Drooliet, but all of a sudden he was grabbed from above.

"Okay, stray, you're coming with me," said Officer Prince, the animal control warden. "And get that dog on a leash," he yelled at the Barkers.

Romeow turned to see what was happening to Turbo, but it wasn't Turbo he was talking about. Turbo was sitting quietly with his tail between his legs. It was Drooliet! Before the Barkers could collar her, Drooliet took off running.

As the animal control truck sped off with Romeow held prisoner inside, everyone scrambled out of the park. The Felinis pursued the van. The Barkers chased after Drooliet. And Benny and Marky took shortcuts through back alleys.

The truck skidded to a stop at its dreaded destination. There was a huge commotion as people, cats and dog arrived. Officer Prince opened the door to Romeow's cage. A split second later Romeow spied Drooliet across the street. She didn't even look for traffic before she crossed. Before Romeow could call out to her, he heard the worst sounds of his life.

First there was screeching, then a dull thud and last a silence as big as the universe. Everyone looked on in disbelief. Drooliet lay motionless in the middle of the street. No one moved. Then Romeow ran towards her.

"Drooliet," Romeow cried, "my love, my wife."

"His wife?" the crowd on the sidewalk gasped.

"We haven't even been married a day," he sobbed as he rubbed her head with his. "I still have to give you your wedding present."

Then Romeow licked Drooliet. He licked her face. He licked her ears. He licked her paws. Slowly, Drooliet opened her eyes. She whimpered, "Oh, Romeow, it's you!"

"Were you expecting a cat in a hat?" Romeow teased.

The crowd cheered. The Barkers hugged the Felinis. The Felinis hugged the Barkers. Turbo, Benny and Marky even high-fived. Officer Prince said it was a miracle and the charges were dropped. A celebration was planned for that evening.

And this time all really *were* welcome.

So how is it that our heroine lived?

From a gift only her true love could give.

This cat gave his dog one of his nine lives.

They shared all the rest at each others' sides.

Felinis and Barkers became fast friends,

And cats and dogs played together again.

Now stories will come and stories will go.

Some wither and die. Some blossom and grow.

Some live in your heart. So don't you forget

The tale of Romeow and Drooliet.